REINACH, JACQUELYN

WAIT ,WAIE ,WAIT ,

	DATE DUE		
NOV 24 1983			
SEP. 25 1986			
MAR. 21 1987			
MAY 2 1987			
MAR. 5 1988			
AUG. 11 1988			
MAY 06 1991			
AUG. 24 1992			
NOV. 28 1992			

TRURO PUPLIC LIBRARY

THIS

SWEET PICKLES ®

BOOK
BELONGS TO

In the Town of Sweet Pickles, the animals get
into and out of pickles because of their all too
human personality traits.

Each of the books in the *Sweet Pickles* series
is about a different pickle.

This book is about having to wait — especially
in long, long lines.

Library of Congress Cataloging in Publication Data

Reinach, Jacquelyn.
   Wait! Wait! Wait!

   (Sweet Pickles series)
   SUMMARY: Responsible Rabbit has trouble coping with
having to wait for things, especially when standing in
line.
   [1. Animals—Fiction.   2. Patience—Fiction]
I. Hefter, Richard.   II. Title.   III. Series.
PZ7.R2747Wai   [E]   80-19072
ISBN 0-937524-00-X

Published by Euphrosyne, Inc.
Sweet Pickles is the registered trademark of
Perle/Reinach/Hefter
Printed in the United States of America
Weekly Reader Books' Edition

Weekly Reader Books presents

WAIT! WAIT! WAIT!

Written by Jacquelyn Reinach
Illustrated by Richard Hefter
Edited by Ruth Lerner Perle

One Saturday morning in the Town of Sweet Pickles, there was a long, long line at the supermarket checkout counter.

Responsible Rabbit tapped his foot and looked at his watch for the seventh time. "I have been *waiting* in this line," he grumbled, "for exactly fourteen minutes and twelve seconds. Why do I have to wait so long?"

"Please try to be patient!" called Enormous Elephant.
"I'm going as fast as I can!"

Elephant was working behind the checkout counter,
ringing up sales and packing groceries into
big brown paper bags.

"Patient!" cried Rabbit. "I have now been waiting in this line for ..." and he looked at his watch for the eighth time, "...exactly fifteen minutes and you want me to be patient!"

"Just wait a minute, Rabbit," smiled Elephant. "Your turn is coming!"

Then the telephone rang. Elephant stopped packing bags. She took her pencil and started writing an order.

"This is terrible!" screamed Rabbit. "There are ten of us waiting to be checked out and she's doing something else. Why do we always have to wait, wait, wait?"

Rabbit's face got very hot and his nose began to twitch. "I want my groceries NOW!" he cried. "I'm already late and I'll miss my bus!"

Elephant hung up the phone. "All right, Rabbit," she said, "you're next."

"Finally!" sighed Rabbit.

Just then Loving Lion came up to the counter. "I can't find the garlic powder," he said.

"I moved all the spices next to the soups," said Elephant. "Here, I'll show you." She walked to the back of the store with Lion.

"HEY! You can't do that!" yelled Rabbit. "It's my turn! I'll miss my bus!"

"I'm sorry," smiled Elephant. "You'll have to be patient."

"I've run out of patience!" shrieked Rabbit. "And I don't want to miss my bus!"

Rabbit added his own grocery prices as fast as he could. Then he jammed his food into a paper bag, tossed the money on the counter and ran out of the market.

Rabbit rushed over to the bus stop. There was a very long line.

"Oh, no!" cried Rabbit. "Not another line!"

"Have a little patience, Rabbit," said Zany Zebra. "It won't be too long a wait if the bus is on time."

"The bus is not on time!" called a voice.
Rabbit looked around.

Yakety Yak was standing in a phone booth on the corner. His taxi was parked at the curb.

"Did you say something?" said Rabbit.

"I said the bus won't be on time," called Yak. "It ran out of gas. I just passed it coming up Sixth Street."

"WHAT???" screamed Rabbit.

"Anyway, as I was saying," said Yak, "the bus ran out of gas, and I'm trying to call Jackal at the gas station to go over to the bus with some gasoline. But there's no answer at the gas station."

"Of course there's no answer at the gas station," snapped Rabbit. "Jackal is still waiting in line at the supermarket! I can't wait any longer, Yak. Take me home in your taxi. Now!"

"Sure," said Yak. "But you'll have to wait awhile. This is my lunch hour."

"Never mind," sighed Rabbit. "I'll just walk home!"

Rabbit hurried across the park. He walked so fast, the groceries in his bag began to jiggle.

Suddenly there was a loud SCRUNCH. The bottom of the bag split open. SPLAT! Rabbit's food went all over the ground...eggs, milk, carrots, cheese...in one big gooey mess.

Just then Positive Pig came skipping along. "Hey, Rabbit!" she smiled. "Don't let a little accident discourage you. It's a beautiful day!"

"No it's not," moaned Rabbit. "This is the worst day of my life!"

"Come on," said Pig. "Here's a nice big plastic shopping bag. Most of this stuff is still good. Let's pick it up and I'll treat you to the movies. There's a great new picture playing. It will make you feel better!"

"I hope so," said Rabbit. "I'm so tired of waiting and waiting!"

Pig and Rabbit walked out of the park and over to the movie theatre.

"Oh, look!" squealed Pig happily. "This must really be a terrific picture. Everyone has come to see it!"

"Oh, no!" screamed Rabbit.

The line at the movie theatre was so long, it went all
the way around the block.

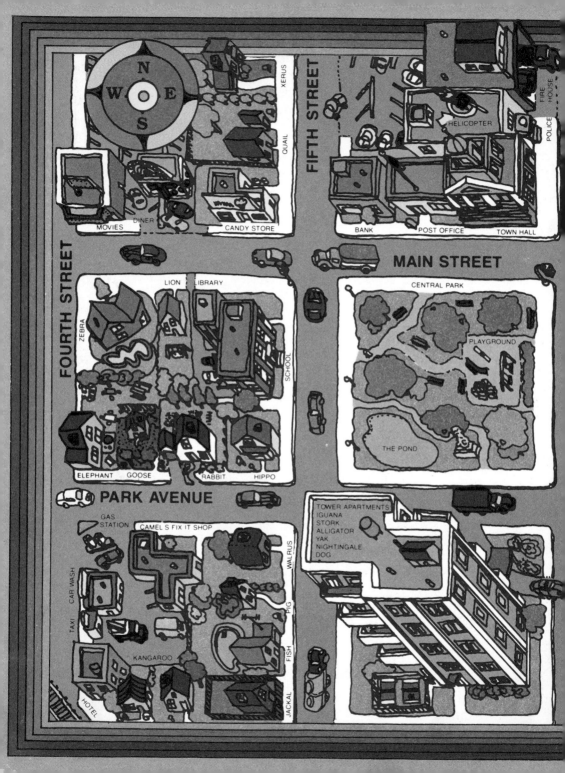